D0438604

PA JINGLEBOB

and the Grabble Gang

Mary Arrigan   Korky Paul

Crabtree Publishing Company
www.crabtreebooks.com

PMB 16A, 350 Fifth Avenue,   616 Welland Avenue,
Suite 3308,   St. Catharines, Ontario
New York, NY 10118   Canada, L2M 5V6

For Conor and Marcella

M.A.

For Oliver David Solomon

K.P.

www.maryarrigan.com

Arrigan, Mary.
Pa Jinglebob and the Grabble Gang / written by Mary Arrigan; illustrated by Korky Paul.
p. cm. -- (Red bananas)
Summary: Although what Pa Jinglebob really likes to do is knit, as sheriff of Buckeroo and
he must take action when the dastardly Mr. Grabble and his gang try to cheat residents out
of their land to build a railroad straight through town.
ISBN-13: 978-0-7787-1074-5 (rlb) -- ISBN-10: 0-7787-1074-2 (rlb)
ISBN-13: 978-0-7787-1090-5 (pbk) -- ISBN-10: 0-7787-1090-4 (pbk)
[1. Sheriffs--Fiction. 2. Swindlers and swindling--Fiction. 3.
Knitting--Fiction. 4. West (U.S.)--Fiction.] I. Paul, Korky, ill. II.
Title. III. Series.
PZ7.A743355Oyp 2006
[Fic]--dc22   2005035772 LC

Published by Crabtree Publishing in 2006
First published in 1988 by Egmont Books Ltd.
Text copyright © Mary Arrigan 2005
Illustrations copyright © Korky Paul 2005
The Author and Illustrator have asserted their moral rights.
Paperback ISBN 0-7787-1090-4
Reinforced Hardcover Binding ISBN 0-7787-1074-2

Contents

Red Bananas

SISSY SHERIFF

Jemima Jinglebob and her great big pa sat
on the porch, rocking in their rocking chairs.
They had just arrived home to Buckaroo after
a vacation in a modern town with hard
sidewalks, brick houses, and pink ice cream. Pa
was busy sharpening sticks with his big knife.

5

"Evenin', Sheriff," said the Mayor as he passed with Mrs. Mayor on their way to the Buckaroo Saloon for their afternoon drink of Mrs. Grace's homemade lemonade. Mrs. Mayor wore a new hat while her husband sported a watch with a gold chain that stretched right across his fat tummy. "You plannin' on catchin' some bears with them thar spears?"

"Nope," replied Pa Jinglebob.

"Howdy, Sheriff," said Cowboy Clarence on his way to have a shampoo and set. His new shirt was made of handpainted satin. "You plannin' on huntin' down some bandits with them little spears?"

"Nope," said Pa Jinglebob. "I'm making new knittin' needles."

7

"Oh, Pa," groaned Jemima. Her pa was the biggest, toughest-looking man in these parts. He was as broad as a brick wall, hairier than a buffalo, and had hands like shovels. But all Pa was interested in was knitting.

"You the sheriff?" a new voice asked.

"Nope," said Pa, casting woolly stitches on to his new knitting needles.

"Yes, Pa. You are the sheriff," said Jemima, thumping her father's big, hairy arm.

"Oh, er, yep," said Pa Jinglebob, looking down at the owner of the new voice.

The stranger was dressed in a long, patched dress, a wide hat, and boots that looked like they'd walked right around the world. She put her hands on her hips and scowled. "Knittin'?" she asked. "I ain't ever seen a knittin' sheriff. Come on, Hercules, we won't get any help here."

"Hold on, Grandma Tendercorns," said a small voice. A small, skinny boy came out from behind the lady's skirt. "I told you this sheriff whops baddies. I heard it from Mo the mailman.

9

He said . . ."

"Enough," said the lady, pulling her hat down over her ears. "I'd never trust a man with knittin' needles. Big sissy."

"Excuse me, lady," said 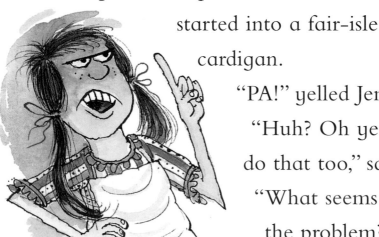 Jemima, standing as tall as she could without falling over. "Just who do you think you're calling a sissy? My pa whops baddies better than anyone in this whole world. Right, Pa?"

"One plain, one purl," muttered Pa, as he started into a fair-isle cardigan.

"PA!" yelled Jemima.

"Huh? Oh yeah, I do that too," said Pa. "What seems to be the problem?"

"It's Osbert J. Grabble," said the small boy. "Tell them, Grandma Tendercorns."

The lady sighed and sat on the porch steps. "Hercules is right," she said. "Osbert J. Grabble is trying to put me and Hercules off our land."

"Can't do that," said Pa, knitting in some red stitches to look good with the purple ones. "Against the law that is."

That darned Grabble!

11

"I know it's against the law," said Grandma. "But he doesn't do law, this Osbert J. Grabble. He just does what he wants. And he wants our land."

"You'd best come in, Mrs. Tendercorns," said Jemima.

Come in.

GREEDY GRABBLE

"So," said Jemima. "Tell us about this crook, Grabble."

Grandma Tendercorns took a rolled-up paper from her pocket.

"I stole that from Grabble's saddlebag," said Hercules proudly.

Grandma Tendercorns spread the paper out on the table. It was a map of all the land for miles around. A red line was drawn right across it.

"See?" she said. "This red line is a railway. He's going to build a railroad right through our land. He's offered us shiny shoes, nice clothes and hats . . ."

"And handpainted satin shirts and a clock with a chain," added Hercules.

"As if we'd sell our land for that garbage," muttered Grandma. "That land belonged to my Pappy Tendercorns, and his pappy and his pappy's pappy. And to think I gave that creep some of my Super-Duper rabbit stew."

Pa Jinglebob leaned closer and squinted at the map. "Why," he said, "that line also goes right through our town, Buckaroo, and the forest beside it."

"It does?" exclaimed Grandma with surprise.

"There, can't you read?" asked Jemima, stabbing the word "Buckaroo" with her finger.

"Nope," replied Grandma. "Ain't no use for letters where we come from"'

"This is very serious," said Pa Jinglebob. "This means that Grabble will try to buy out the town of Buckaroo."

"Pa!" exclaimed Jemima. "Clothes, clocks chained to tummies, handpainted satin shirts – I think he's already started!"

"Darn it," said Pa Jinglebob. "We should never have left town to go on that vacation. Make some posters, sweet Jemima. We need to call a meeting."

"If we're not too late," groaned Jemima.

GROTTY GIFTS

"Listen up, folks," said Jemima later. The whole population of Buckaroo had gathered in Mr. and Mrs. Grace's saloon.

They were dressed in fancy clothes and shiny shoes. Even Not-Nice-Nellie, ex-bandit, who now had a cleaning business in Buckaroo, sported new feather dusters in her ex-six-gun holsters. Everyone was talking at once, making a terrible racket.

"I SAID LISTEN!" yelled Jemima. "MY PA HAS SOMETHING TO SAY."

Pa knitted the last stitch and bit off the wool.

"Did you folks know that a man called Osbert J. Grabble is planning to build a railroad right here in Buckaroo?" he asked, spitting out a bit of woolly fuzz.

There was a noise of shuffling feet and everyone looked at their hands, the ceiling, their bellybuttons – anywhere except at Sheriff Pa Jinglebob. Nobody answered.

"Nice man, Mr. Grabble," said Cowboy Clarence, wiping the runny paint from his shirt off his arm.

There was a crack of breaking wood and someone fell to the floor. "Ouch!"

Mr. Grabble gave me those new wooden chairs for my saloon!

"You see, Sheriff," said Mr. Bones as he polished his new undertaker's hat and didn't notice the black ink that stuck to his forehead. "While you were away he came and told us he was building a railroad near here that would make Buckaroo a rich town with hard sidewalks, brick buildings, and pink ice cream."

"Did he show you the plans?" asked Pa.

"Er, harummph," began Mr. Mayor. "There was no need, Sheriff," he said. "He told us not to bother about the stupid words."

"Sillies!" said Jemima. "Show them the plans, Pa."

When Pa held up the plans for all to see, there was a huge gasp.

"That . . . that railroad doesn't go *around* our town. It goes right THROUGH it!" said Mrs. Mayor.

GASP!

"That's right," said Jemima. "Looks like he intends to knock down the whole town and the forest."

Crack! Four more people fell through the new chairs.

Just then the door burst open and a breathless cowboy came running in. "It's him!" he cried. "It's that nice Mr. Grabble. He's heading this way with two of his men."

"Eh, mebbe you'd, eh, hide the knittin',
Sheriff," whispered Mr. Mayor.

"Nope," said Pa Jinglebob, tucking his
knitting under his arm and following
everyone as they rushed out to meet the man
who was about to take over Buckaroo.

BYE-BYE BUCKAROO?

Outside, the thundering of hooves got louder and from the middle of the dust cloud, a man with a wobbly belly, a shiny suit, and a cigar emerged.

"Afternoon, Mr. Grabble!" said Mr. Mayor, bowing so low his new breeches split. "Tell the sheriff that you're not going to knock down our town."

"Afraid so," said Mr. Grabble. "This here town is right in the middle of my new railroad. But I'm a fair and decent man. I have a nice place all ready for you," he went on, pointing towards the scrubby land beyond Buckaroo.

One plain, one purl.

"But . . . but that's the desert," spluttered Mr. Mayor.

"Yep," said Osbert J. Grabble. "Lovely and warm. Lots of sunshine and tons of sand for the children to play with."

Everyone began talking at once.

"Ain't nothin' anyone can do," laughed Mr. Grabble. "Especially a sissy knittin' sheriff," he snickered to his two sidekicks. "You all signed these papers to say that I'd given you those fancy clothes and stuff. What you really did was sign away Buckaroo, the forest, and the Tendercorns Ranch."

Grandma Tendercorns was outraged. "You tricked me! I thought I was signing to say I would never sign away our ranch."

"He can't take our town, can he, Sheriff?" asked Miss Brown.

"Yep," said Pa, unrolling some white wool.

"WHAT!" everyone roared.

"If you signed your names and took stuff, then the town is his," explained Pa.

"But we thought we were signing a thank you note," groaned Mr. Mayor. "Nobody bothered to read the words."

Mr. Grabble chuckled again. "Let's go, boys," he said to his sidekicks. "We'll be back tomorrow with our demolition gang to knock Buckaroo to dust. We'll be starting with that forest."

With whoops and cheers, the trio disappeared over the hill.

SISSY SHERIFF!

Maybe we'll get him to knit some pretty covers for our hot water bottles.

SUPER-DUPER STEW

"We're finished," groaned Mr. Mayor. "All is lost."

"Looks like it," said Pa Jinglebob. "TWO plain, one purl. And mebbe a bit of a twist."

"Knitting!" muttered the townspeople, switching their attention to Pa. "We're about to lose our town and you just sit there knittin'."

Mutter, mutter, grumble, grumble.

"Hold on there, people!" shouted Jemima. "You greedy bunch signed away the town in exchange for cheap gifts that are falling apart, and you have the nerve to blame my pa!"

"She has a point," said Mr. Bones.

"I'm angrier than a bear sittin' on a
cactus," muttered Not-Nice-Nellie, waving
her new feather dusters. "Why don't I just go
after that varmint, me and my boys," she
nodded towards the team of ex-bandits who
now helped her to run her cleaning business.
"We'll knock that oily grin off his face."

"No rough stuff," said Pa Jinglebob. "Go
home, everyone. Except for my Jemima,
Grandma Tendercorns, Hercules, and you,
Miss Brown, ma'am."

"Jemima, my sweet," said Pa, as the people slunk away. "You and Hercules get lots and lots of buttons. And, Miss Brown," he went on, "bring every kid in Buckaroo to the schoolhouse."

"And what about me, Sheriff?" asked Grandma Tendercorns.

"You'll make up one of your Super-Duper rabbit stews," he said.

You do have a plan, my brave pa!

WHOPPING BADDIES

Next morning, many riders, all with mean faces, dirty boots, and no manners, thundered into town.

Yee-ha!

Quick! Get Pa!

"Call the sheriff," Mrs. Grace ordered her husband. He ran to the schoolhouse. "They've gone!" he shouted. "That cowardly sheriff has done a runner with all of our kids."

"And some of our horses," added Cowboy Clarence, flicking his gelled hair.

Osbert J. Grabble hooted with laughter. "Wise man, your knittin' sheriff," he said. "He wouldn't want to face the might of Osbert J. Grabble and his gang. Come on, boys. There's a whole forest to be knocked down."

Jemima Jinglebob was standing at the edge of the forest. "I wouldn't go in there, Mr. Grabble," she said. "It's dark in that thar forest. And scary. You and your boys should be careful."

"Scary?" laughed Osbert J. Grabble. "Me and my boys don't scare, no siree."

By now the people of Buckaroo had arrived on the scene.

Osbert J. Grabble frowned. "Go find your sissy sheriff. Is he away knittin' some curtains for your new desert homes? Haw haw."

His men picked up their axes and picnic
baskets and ran into the forest, laughing like
itchy hyenas.

"Might as well go home," said Mrs. Grace.
"While we still have homes to go to."

"Sshhh," said Jemima. "Wait."

"See here, little lady . . ." began Mrs. Mayor.
She broke off as there were terrified screams
and yells coming from the forest.

"I warned you,"
said Jemima. "Scary
place, that forest."

HELP!

HELP!

Suddenly Grabble's men appeared.
"Aaaaggghhh!" they cried. "Help!"
"Huh!" cried Osbert J. Grabble. "Git back
in that thar forest, you men."

Throwing down their axes and picnic baskets, the men jumped on their horses and disappeared in a cloud of dust.

"Come back!" roared Osbert J. Grabble. "There's no such thing as ghosts." He broke off as the shrieking and screeching from the dark forest grew closer. His horse reared up in fear. The paper with all the signatures of the people of Buckaroo fell from the saddlebag. Quick as a flash, Jemima snatched it.

Got it!

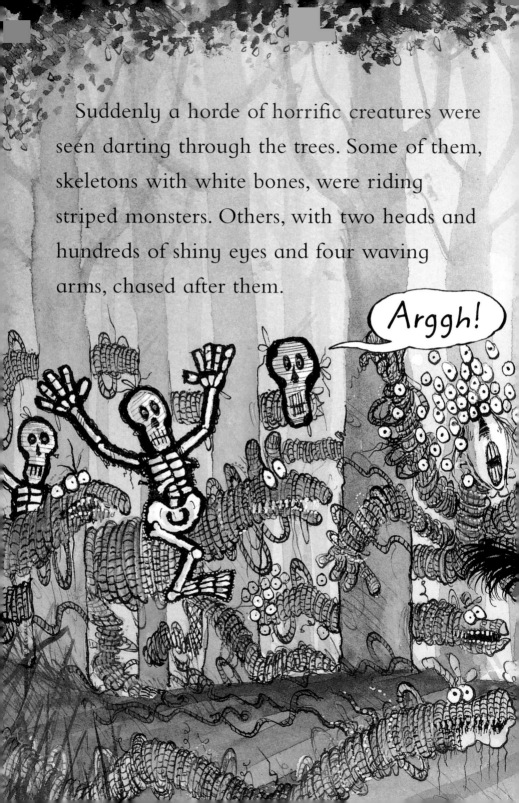

Suddenly a horde of horrific creatures were seen darting through the trees. Some of them, skeletons with white bones, were riding striped monsters. Others, with two heads and hundreds of shiny eyes and four waving arms, chased after them.

"You can keep your scary forest," croaked Osbert J. Grabble. "I'm off. Wait, boys. Don't leave me!"

As the terrifying creatures emerged, laughing and giggling, the people looked at them with amazement.

They're our kids!

Sure enough, some of the children were dressed in scary knitted outfits with lots of shiny buttons sewn on. Others, wearing plain and purl skeleton outfits, were riding horses that wore striped, woolly coats.

"That was fun," laughed Hercules, throwing a fair-isle knit snake in the air.

"Well done, team," said Pa Jinglebob as he and Miss Brown joined them.

Good work, kids!

Yes!

Later on, at a party in the Buckaroo
Saloon, Mrs. Grace planted a big kiss on Pa
Jinglebob's head. "You've saved our town,
Pa," she said.

"And the Tendercorns Ranch," added
Hercules proudly.

"Not RANCH," smiled Grandma Tendercorns. "COUNTRY RESTAURANT. Mrs. Grace here says my stew is the best darn stew in the whole West, so me and Hercules will be opening The Tendercorns Classy Nosh House next week."

Everyone cheered.

"We owe it all to our sheriff, Pa Jinglebob," said Mr. Grace.

"Shucks," said Pa, blushing. "It was the TWO plain, one purl and a bit of a twist that did it."

"That's my pa," said Jemima. "Still the fastest knitter in the West."